OCOTZINALLI

and Other New Britain Stories

PABLO HELGUERA

OCOTZINALLI

and Other New Britain Stories

Jorge Pinto Books
New York

JORGE
PINTO
BOOKS

Ocotzinalli (and Other New Britain Stories)

© Pablo Helguera

Edition © Jorge Pinto Books Inc.

ISBN 13: 978-1-934978-70-2
ISBN: 1-934978-70-1
Edited by Kristina O'Leary
Design: Charles King: www.ckmm.com
Cover design and all illustrations © Pablo Helguera

**NEW BRITAIN
MUSEUM OF
AMERICAN ART**

New Britain, Connecticut

INTRODUCTION

Over the years, I have often gravitated to obscure or little known stories of people, ghosts, or past events. I am interested in the lives of historical and sometimes nearly forgotten individuals—from eccentric inventors to spiritual leaders, from utopian thinkers to hermits—who have come to inspire my own research and writing. They have included the Italian philosopher Giulio Camillo, who built a "memory theater" in which all the things of the world could be known; Florence Foster Jenkins, a wealthy amateur opera singer with great motivation but no sense of pitch—or self-awareness—who funded her own extravagant performances; and Horace Wells, the Hartford dentist who pioneered the use of anesthesia and died in tragic circumstances. For two decades I have been interested in the history of the Shakers, a Christian sect that became the longest and most successful socialistic experiment in the United States, spanning four centuries, but represented by only two surviving members today; and Friedrick Fröebel, the German educator who invented Kindergarten and died without seeing the success of his educational system. I also once wrote about Ward Jackson, the life-long archivist of the Guggenheim Museum with whom I once shared an office in the 1990s. Ever a shy man, Ward was an abstract painter who had been friends with artists including Willem de Kooning, Dan Flavin, and Robert Ryman, whom he later told me about as we got to know each other. He revered the museum where he worked, calling it a "temple of the spirit," a term used by its first director, Hilla Rebay.

In developing stories about these individuals and occurrences, I have always had to consider why they mattered to me. The answer, I later realized, had to do perhaps with how their narratives resonate with my own personal experience. My family, from both my father's side (the Helgueras) and my mother's (the Lizaldes), happens to be full of utopians and intrepids, some of whom succeeded to a degree and many of whom did not. They include my great-great grandfather Trinidad García de la Cadena, governor of the state of Zacatecas, Mexico, in the 19th century, who rose up in arms—unsuccessfully—against the dictator Porfirio Díaz and was executed; my grandmother's father, who was the first to bring the then advanced technology of typewriters into Zacatecas in the early 1900s; my grand-uncle Andrés Helguera, who invented a tortilla warmer that never took off (an item that I still think has a future); and my own grandfather Ignacio Helguera, a self-made businessman and patriarch of the family who yearned to be a novelist and produced many self-published books that had few to no readers. Ignacio's editions remained in boxes in our family house many years after his passing, and my uncle eventually used the books as fuel for his furnace, saying that he was doing my grandfather a favor. This uncle was also an inventor and for decades owned a tiny factory that produced *estopa* (a material derived from hemp fiber and utilized to seal pipe junctures) that slowly ground to a halt as the demand for this material lessened over the years.

In today's world in which we seem to be constantly bombarded by corporate narratives of success regarding audacious individuals who build commercial empires from scratch, rags-to-riches stories, miraculous diets and body transformations—I am instead interested in the stories of those who, although visionary thinkers, never experienced success, public acknowledgment, or redemption in life, but who, with the passage of time, have eventually been recognized for their achievements and tribulations. This was the case of Giulio Camillo, who constructed a Renaissance-era equivalent of a contemporary search engine, or Florence Foster Jenkins, who was a performance artist at heart long before that notion existed.

I have always, moreover, been intrigued by the subject of the outsider, being that I myself have lived this condition in many ways, as observer of the world, as an artist, and as an immigrant. This book is the record of trying to make sense of three stories of New Britain, Connecticut, that provoked such interests.

In 2017, I was invited by Lisa Williams from the New Britain Museum of American Art to propose an exhibition for their galleries. Over a period of several months I traveled to New Britain to learn about the history of the city and the museum's holdings. Encountering the museum's remarkable collection of Shaker-made objects was very meaningful to me, particularly as the legacy of this religious and social group has inspired my work in the past.

The industrial history of New Britain also resonated with me in the way it connected to my own family's entrepreneurial endeavors.

Similarly, I have long been interested in the relationship between biography and place, and the saying, truthful or not, that "geography is destiny." When I learned that Sol LeWitt—a towering figure of American art—grew up a few blocks away from the museum, I wanted to learn more about his story.

Working with a museum that possesses some of the most important illustration holdings in the United States, including the nation's largest collection of images created for pulp fiction novels, was a uniquely valuable experience. Merging visual and literary narratives, the museum's collection of pulp art inspired the format of this small exhibition, which consisted of three illustrated stories, presented along with some of the artworks and objects that inspired them. This accompanying book contains the three narratives of the exhibition as well as the illustrations that I created for them.

As a Latin American artist with a literary background, I am inevitably familiar with the legacy of writers like Carlos Fuentes, Gabriel García Márquez, and Juan Rulfo, whose stories often describe worlds in which time, memory, and reality intermix to produce unique and particular narrative experiences. It was the language that I felt appropriate to utilize in dialogue with the tradition of fantastical writing addressed in this exhibition—from Mark Twain's time travel novel *A Connecticut Yankee in King Arthur's Court* to pulp fiction novels that describe extraordinary tales of intergalactic travel and futuristic scenarios.

I am grateful to the time that the New Britain Museum of American Art staff have generously given me to explore their collections and the history of their city. I owe special thanks to museum trustee Stephen Miller, who generously shared his vast knowledge of the Shaker collection, and to Karen Hudkins for introducing me to the industrial history of New Britain. I am especially grateful to Lisa Williams and the museum's director, Min Jung Kim, who shepherded this project from the very start with great enthusiasm and determination. Last but not least, I thank Kristina O'Leary, who provided much needed editing support for this small book.

Pablo Helguera
Brooklyn, New York, February 2019

The Gift Drawing of Sister Alison Parr

Leap and shout

the living building

Christ is in his glory come

Cast your horizon mothers children
see what
glory fills the room

Full of glory out in motion skipping like the lambs in hay

dancing in
the
sweet devotion.

all the
blessed virgins
play

Once it was our best devotion in our guild to even pray.

to our
father

while our
notion

fixed him

bar above
the
sky

There we strove to stretch
our senses
when we try
to sing or pray

Now our father and
our mother
are with us
from day to day

The Shakers, more properly known as the United Society of Believers in Christ's Second Appearing, were a Christian sect that came to Colonial America in the 18th Century, lead by a woman referred to as Mother Ann Lee. Ruled by a life of communitarian work and simple living, the Shakers were pacifists who believed in the equality of the sexes and held a strong work ethic summarized by Mother Ann's dictum, "hands to work, hearts to God." Today, the Shakers are associated with their perfectly crafted furniture and oval boxes; their villages in New England, now preserved as historical landmarks and museums; and their worship dances—the same dances that centuries ago earned them the moniker "Shaking Quakers" for which they became known.

The golden age of the Shaker faith took place between 1820 and 1860, when their communities reached their highest numbers. It was in that period, specifically during the spring of 1837, when a series of events took all the Shaker communities by surprise. During those months, several Shakers began experiencing deep spiritual revelations, often entering ecstatic states in which the experienced visions that were often later translated into a song, dance, or what they described as a "gift drawing."

These visions initially occurred in Watervliet, New York, the first village settled by the Shakers, and soon spread to the other communities throughout Connecticut and Massachusetts, and as far as Kentucky and Indiana. The period would be eventually remembered as "The Era of Manifestations."

Most significantly, it was almost always young women who would enter into a convulsive state and later declare they had had these spiritual revelations.

These unusual encounters were received with both puzzlement and excitement by the Shakers—excitement about witnessing a clear sign of God's communication with the mortal world, but puzzlement, and perhaps also a certain jealousy among the elders, because it was the younger women, not the leadership, who received these powerful visions.

One of those who received such visions was sister Alison Parr.

Sister Alison was a member of the vibrant Enfield Shaker community. Visitors to the small New England town of Enfield, as well as those newly arrived, would quickly become acquainted with the Shakers and the important role they played in daily life there. While living in strict separation from "the world," the three Shaker families of Enfield nonetheless practiced commerce with the local residents and were a reliable resource for many of their needs, including schooling for their children.

The three Shaker families strictly adhered to the rules established by Mother Ann. According to those rules, Shaker men and women were not allowed to be alone together, and would observe strict separation even in their living quarters, where there were separate doors and stairs for each sex. Despite this strict separation they all worked, dined, and worshiped together.

People "from the world" outside Shaker society were not allowed access to daily Shaker life, but they were welcome to attend their Sunday meetings. It was only during those meetings that a non-Shaker could obtain a glimpse of the Shaker faith. Their meetings included songs as well as elaborately choreographed group dances with names such as the Hollow Square, the Square Step, Circular Square and Compound dance. Brothers and sisters would dance together in symmetric and opposing groups, never touching one another (as this was prohibited) but always in perfect coordination.

Sister Alison joined the Enfield Shakers as a child. She was born around 1820 in New York. When she was very young, both her parents died of an infectious disease. Her extended family took her to be cared for by the Enfield Shakers. This is how, as an orphan, little Alison joined the Shaker faith. She was a slight young woman, by all accounts incredibly hard working and dedicated to all her tasks and responsibilities. Her delicate, fawn-like appearance concealed her deep resilience. Mostly quiet, she was often pensive and loved taking care of the farm animals and staring at the glorious sunsets of the "chosen Vale," as the Shakers used to describe the location of their community. She was particularly fond of, and dedicated to, the many Shaker dances that were performed at the meeting house. Being such an enthusiast of these activities she would often be asked to demonstrate to others. She knew every dance and every song, and took pains to perform them with great precision.

One morning, Sister Alison was working at the dairy farm when she suddenly collapsed to the ground. While she was being assisted by other Shakers, her body started to convulse. She lay in bed for three weeks with high fevers. At night, she experienced powerful visions, some of which lasted several hours. At times she would open her big blue eyes and start speaking in a trembling voice, seemingly addressing an angelical presence in the room.

The local doctor was unable to determine the cause of her illness. —At one point it was believed she had cholera. There were rumors that she would not survive.

Nonetheless, sister Alison's health did improve. Her fever subsided and with each passing day she regained her strength. With the help of sister Ruth, who took care of the sick, she eventually was able to take short strolls and sit outside of the meeting house in the mornings. She was unusually silent in this period. After several weeks, she fully recovered and resumed her duties in the community.

Following her recovery, Sister Alison started speaking of the powerful visions she experienced during her illness, which she recalled vividly and would discuss in minute detail. She had seen images of large singing trees, populated with angels, and of a deep valley where "heavenly spirits" lived. She saw powerful images of the heavens where the stars lined up in circular fashion, slowly moving in perfect harmony as the Shakers did in their dances.

It was not long before she obtained large sheets of paper and began illustrating her elaborate visions in beautiful, detailed drawings. Shaker Laws, however, dictate that "no maps, charts, and no pictures or paintings, shall ever be hung up in your dwelling-rooms, shops, or office. And no pictures of paintings set in frames, with glass before them, shall ever be among you." So what was to be done with Sister Alison's drawings?

Could it be possible that this display prohibition by the Shaker leadership stemmed from their discomfort at not being given the gift of drawing themselves?

Following Shaker rule, Sister Alison Parr kept all of her gift drawings stowed away in a secret place, where they remained for half a century. In one of her letters, directed to a family member in her old age, she wrote:

> *When I was young I was visited by angels who gave me the gift of heavenly visions. I might never be able to fully explain what I saw, but I attempted to illustrate those visions on paper, to the best of my ability. Those drawings are very important to me, but sometimes I wonder if anyone else should ever see them. I decided to keep them hidden, and only every so often I retrieve them to look at them and remember the beauty of those visions.*

When Sister Alison passed away, in the late 1800s, the number of Shaker communities had already begun to decline, as it was the case for the entirety of the membership of the Shaker faith. In the early 1920s, when the Shaker community in Enfield was reduced to a handful of members, they made the decision to leave and join the Canterbury Shaker village in New Hampshire.

The Shaker houses were sold and their contents vacated. Boxes of books and hymnals were sent to a local library.

Sometime in the 1920's, the daughter of the librarian in Enfield, who was helping to sort out the Shaker materials, opened the boxes and discovered one of Sister Alison's drawings.

It is said she was immediately fascinated by the drawing and took it home, staring at it for several hours that night. It is also said that the following day she woke with a high fever and experienced convulsions, and spoke in tongues while embracing the drawing.

It is unclear what became of the librarian's daughter. Some say that she never recovered from the experience. There are rumors she joined a religious order. It is said that the rest of Sister Alison Parr's drawings are kept in a restricted archive for scholars to study, accompanied by a warning, particularly for young women, to refrain from looking at these mysteriously powerful artworks.

I Love to see the Wheels

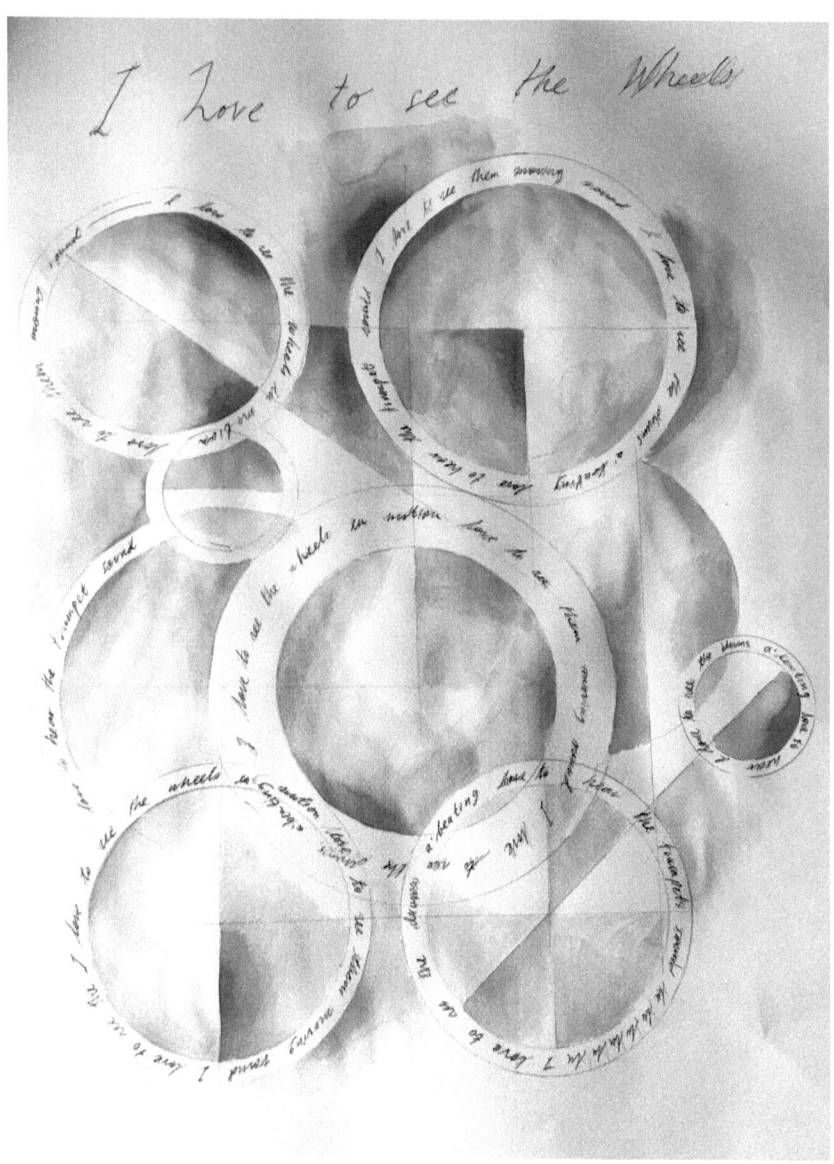

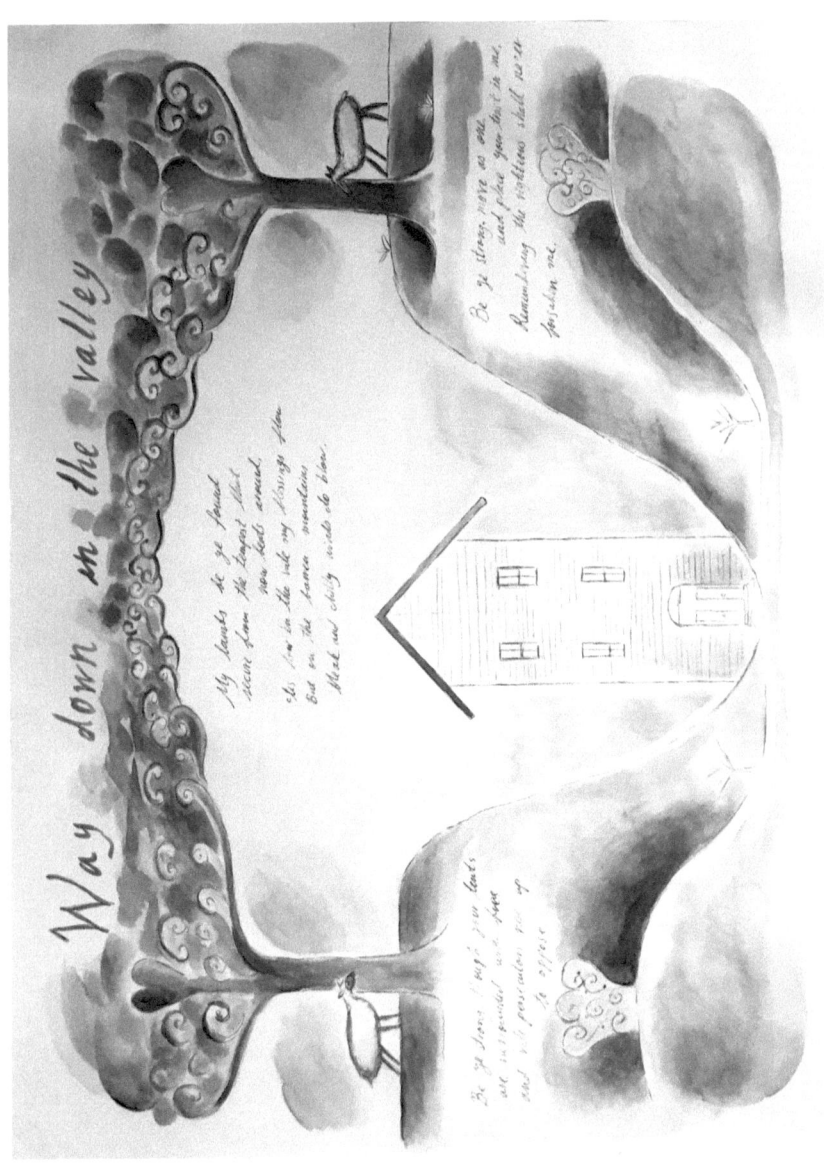

19

Ocotzinalli

On a cold winter morning, I stood in front of the old narrow building on Sunnyledge Street, unsure as to whether I was in the right place. I looked again at the crumpled piece of paper that I had received from a friend of Mrs. Casey Ripleton's daughter, and saw that the addressed matched exactly.

I was there to research Mrs. Ripleton's collection. She was known to own a large group of objects related to New Britain's industrial history—a collection that promised to be very valuable for an exhibition I was putting together at that time. She came from a storied family in the area who had played an important role at the turn of the 19th century here, producing ball bearings and other machine parts.

A young woman timidly opened the large door. I assumed she was Mrs. Ripleton's daughter, but she appeared to be at odds with this house, as much as I was. Was she her assistant? She led me up the dark, rickety staircase of the old Victorian house. Portraits covered the walls. Ancestors, I assumed. Bookshelves lined the walls absolutely everywhere, with rows of very old books that seemed as if no one had ever read them. The musky smell typical of old libraries made them even more present. I remembered the monumental 15-volume history of France that my grandfather once purchased and proudly displayed at his home. Printed in 1885, it remains unopened to this day.

A large suit of arms stood in a dark corner. Windows cast a jaundiced tint through the entire house. The stairs led to a very large room, incongruent to the size of the house.

Mrs. Ripleton, an older lady in her late 80s, was sitting at the end of the room in a large wicker chair. She seemed almost immobile, like a spectral image, hardly acknowledging my presence.

I walked toward her, trying to be as polite as possible.

"Mrs. Ripleton, I am Mr. Helguera. We spoke on the phone about your collection."

"Yes. It's there," she said, pointing past me to a door. "Take a look and just tell me what you want to borrow."

She pointed me to a room that resembled an oversized attic. It was strangely shaped and absolutely enormous. It reminded me of the warehouse of the opera of Bellas Artes in Mexico City, a place in which one can find props, furniture, curtains, and objects from 90 years of opera productions in that theater. In this room were several vitrines with a variety of objects, mostly old pieces of machinery, piles of cast-iron wheels that belonged to some kind of assembly line structure, and many crates containing rusted machine parts. I had been told that Mrs. Ripleton's father, after closing his family's factory, had kept many pieces of equipment with the intention of creating an Industry and Technology Museum in New Britain— a project that, for one reason or another, never came to fruition. I even saw a dusty sign with the grandiose letters "The New Britain National Museum of Industry," I assumed an attempt to promote the museum project in the city.

I came back several times to examine Mrs. Ripleton's collection. I had a large green notebook in which I meticulously kept the description of every object. The exercise became routine after a few times: the young woman would open the door and lead me to the storage area, always as if I had never been there before.

After our first meeting, I didn't encounter Ms. Ripleton again, but I had the distinct feeling that she was in the house. I once imagined her watching me work from a concealed peephole in another room.

It was an arduous task to review all the objects. They were dirty, dusty, and very heavy. I did my best to create an inventory of what was available. I will never forget the odd aromas of machine oil and orange-scented cleaner that permeated the house.

Large piles of boxes blocked access to the objects in the back. I slowly made my way through most of the boxes, until I found a crate hidden behind an upright piano. It was sealed and on top, a single word had been written in shaky handwriting in pencil,

OCOTZINALLI

The crate appeared as if it had been sealed for a long time. I tried to look for Mrs. Ripleton to ask her about it but she was nowhere in sight. In the end, given that I had permission to go over the collection, I decided I had permission to open that crate.

It took quite some time to do so; it appeared that it had not been opened in decades.

When I finally opened the lid, I perceived an earthy smell, and felt a breeze of cold air. Standing before me was a statue made of carved stone. Its porous material suggested to me that it was made of volcanic rock, and the effigy—a kneeling woman with a headdress and eyes in the shape of flowers— appeared to be a representation of a pre-Columbian goddess of some sort.

I saw Mrs. Ripleton's assistant only when I entered or left the house. That day, as I was exiting the house, I addressed her:

"I have a question: I found a statue inside a crate that said 'Ocotzinalli' and wanted to know more about the object. Could you please ask Mrs. Ripleton about it?"

The young assistant looked at me with terror in her face. I was taken aback by her reaction.

"Is everything okay?" I asked.

"That crate should have never been opened," she said, as she closed the door.

The next day I received a curt email from Mrs. Ripleton's daughter saying that her mother had decided against lending any objects for the exhibition She requested that I not return to the house.

I was perplexed by the request. The only possible ex-planation I could find for this was that my last question regarding the crate in the corner, and perhaps my opening it, had prompted this reaction. So, I wrote a response to Mrs. Ripleton's daughter:

Dear Ms. Ripleton,

I am very sorry to hear that your mother would prefer if I did not return to her home. I am afraid I must have made an inappropriate inquiry during my last visit regarding a crate that I saw in the corner, and which I also opened.

If her request is related to this inquiry, I sincerely apologize for causing any discomfort and will, of course, refrain from any further contact.

Sincerely,
P.H.

A few months went by, during which I continued my research visiting other private collections, although the mystery behind that crate was never far from my mind.

That spring, I received a call from Mrs. Ripleton's daughter.

"My mother would like to see you tomorrow, if you have time."

I was in New York City and not planning to travel to New Britain any time soon. However, the urgency of the message seemed to convey that this needed to happen right away, so I made the necessary plans to travel the next day to New Britain.

Mrs. Ripleton was waiting for me in the room where I had first met her. She now had an oxygen tank and a breathing tube. Beside her, the crate lay open, showing the Pre-Columbian statue inside.

Mrs. Ripleton started speaking without greeting me. I realized that it was the first time she actually looked at me. I thought of her eyes when she must have been young, and I also thought, simultaneously, of the flower-shaped eyes of the statue.

"The other day," she started, "I had a health incident."

As she paused, I could hear the low wheezing sound of the oxygen tank. "I fell to the floor, and couldn't move. I went to the doctor, who is now looking at my heart."

She paused for a second.

"It is not a coincidence, you see. I am required to tell you her story, because that is what *she* wants."

She pointed at the stone figure.

I was utterly confused about what I had just heard, but did not utter a word. Mainly I tried to focus and continued to listen while the frail woman slowly started telling the story, which I will attempt to summarize here.

Her grandfather, Eleazar Ripleton, built a ball-bearing factory in New Britain. He was an orphan, a self-made man. He never went to school, but he had street smarts and was entirely self-taught. He was ambidextrous, and possessed a scientific mind. He was very good at math and studied engineering. "I think he was a very idealistic person, if you ask me," Mrs. Ripleton said. "But he was fearless and would try anything, never worrying about the consequences."

This allowed him to start a successful business with the help of his mentor, Mr. Elmer Shipley, who treated him as a son. Upon Shipley's passing, Ripleton eventually took over Mr. Shipley's business and built his factory from it.

Although he didn't go to school, he always had a passion for learning, which led him to travel the world. He traveled to Southern Europe when he was young, spending time in Portugal, Spain, and Italy. When his business started to grow, he aspired to be a learned man, admiring, as he did, people of the upper echelons of society who had the opportunities of youth that he didn't have. For this reason he feverishly started amassing a wide variety of books, including many in other languages. He was very curious about, and interested in Hispanic culture, often acquiring artworks, decorative items and textiles from Spain, Mexico, and Peru. He was fascinated by Baroque Spanish art, and purchased a number of wooden saints, mostly from colonial era Mexico, that he cherished. He became a customer of several antique sellers in the area. He bought medieval armor, an 18th century tapestry depicting the burial of Philip I of Castile, and a giant talavera ceramic pot from colonial Puebla.

One day, one of his antique sellers brought him a very unique item: a statuette of the Aztec goddess Ocotzinalli. It was unclear how this statue had made its way to Connecticut, but, as Mrs. Ripleton recalled, a soldier who had fought in the Mexican-American War had found it in the basement of an abandoned convent near Mexico City where his garrison was stationed and had decided to bring it home.

Mr. Ripleton found the statuette fascinating and decided to place it in his office, overlooking the second floor assembly line of his factory.

Mr. Ripleton forgot about the statue for a while, but every now and then he had the feeling that he was being observed—a feeling, of course, that he deemed absurd, in spite of how recurrent it was.

One day he needed to meet a deadline for a major delivery of products, but he did not have enough money to purchase the equipment and pay for the labor for a quick turnaround. Jokingly, he addressed the statue, "Please help me, Aztec goddess. I need money to come out of nowhere."

Moments later, a friend who had just received a large inheritance called on him. He wanted to invest it in a business. "I thought of you," he said. "Do you need a partner?" More lucky episodes began to come in quick procession, and Ripleton started to suspect that Ocotzinalli was listening to him—a feeling that was both troubling and exciting, as he was, by nature, very suspicious of the supernatural. Yet, he found that every time he explained his problems to Ocotzinalli, some event would happen that would prove beneficial to him.

One day it happened that Ripleton was in another serious bind. He had obtained a large loan from the bank to purchase additional machinery, but the investment had not gone according to plan. He was behind in payments with the lender and they were threatening to take possession of his business. One night, as he was leaving his office, he looked at the goddess and offered a proposal: "If you help me," he said, "I will bring you flowers every day."

The next day he received a call from a weapons manufacturer. The United States was entering World War I which meant that a massive amount of machinery for war equipment would be needed. An order was submitted.

Ripleton's business boomed. His factory grew three-fold

during the roaring 20's. He did buy flowers to the goddess and ensured that they were refreshed on a regular basis. By the end of that decade, Ripleton was a rich man. He introduced an electrically powered engine that was considered state-of-the-art, and which comprised a web of thick cables that would sort parts in an automated capacity, much faster than what had been accomplished in the past by human hands.

Nonetheless, a few years into his business bonanza, Ripleton forgot about the stone figure in the factory and it became dusty, simply sitting there, seemingly forlorn.

One day, a reporter doing a story on the metal industry in New Britain visited the factory. Ripleton was giving the reporter a tour of the facilities, when the reporter spotted the statue of Ocotzinalli and inquired about it.

"Oh, that's a figurine I got a long time ago, some kind of Mexican goddess," Mr. Ripleton replied. "When I was young and desperate I thought it had magical powers and would bring me good fortune. Isn't that funny?"

"I take it you don't believe in magic now?" asked the reporter.

"When you are young and naïve," Mr. Ripleton said, "you believe the forces of Fate are dependent on luck that the spirits can guide you to success. But all that is nonsense. We are alone in this world. It is hard work that brings rewards, not the belief in bogus spirits."

The account of what immediately followed varies, depending on who you ask—the journalist or Mr. Ripleton's assistant, who witnessed the interview. According to the journalist, around that moment in their conversation, one of the thick electrical cables from a new machine under which Mr. Ripleton stood, disengaged and fell on his head, discharging a brutal electric current and killing him instantly. We will never know for sure, but Mr. Ripleton's assistant swore that, while the workers ran toward the inert body, he saw the sculpture of Ocotzinalli glow bright red for a few moments, as if it were made of volcanic lava.

Mrs. Ripleton gestured to her assistant. She closed the crate with the Aztec statue. She took a moment, as she seemed short of breath. Then she added:

"Ever since I heard that story, when I was a young girl, I have been terrified by this statue. I am not a religious person. But I believe that one should never project anger or fear toward others. I know that she and I are part of this place. In a way, we both happen to be here due to reasons outside of our control. We are at peace. But I can't ever let her go, nor take her out. I have to live with her, in this way. I know that is what she wants."

I left Mrs. Ripleton shortly afterward. I tried to walk in the crusty snow outside of her house, thinking of every word she had said. There were so many questions floating in my head.

The name Ocotzinalli kept resounding in my mind.

A few days ago, I contacted my high school friend's father, an Aztec scholar, anthropologist, and archaeologist who teaches at the National University of Mexico. I wanted to know if he was familiar with that name.

In an email, he generously explained:

"Ocotzinalli is the name of an Aztec deity. She is considered a minor deity, the sister of Xochiquetzal, the goddess of the arts and fertility. Ocotzinalli was the older sister of Xochiquetzal and always felt ignored by her parents, who seemed to always give their attention to her sister. Ocotzinalli grew to have a volatile character, always resentful of Xochiquetzal. One day, during a quarrel with her sister, Ocotzinalli left the house never to return. She is considered a powerful protector of those who feel lost or are unloved and is generally seen as a deity of the underdogs, but she can also be dangerous, as she punishes those who are disloyal."

I was at home when I read this email. Spring was coming. People were already hanging pastel-colored decorations to celebrate Easter. Looking out the window of my apartment, I saw the flowers planted in February by my neighbor, an elderly lady devoted to tending our yard. All of them were blooming in many colors, red, blue, but mostly yellow. For a moment, I wondered if those flowers were eyes, looking at my life, inspecting my movements, making sure I followed in my acts and decisions a particularly required rhythm of life that must not, under any circumstances, be disturbed by our excessive requirements, and by our many inconsiderate demands to our life and our destiny.

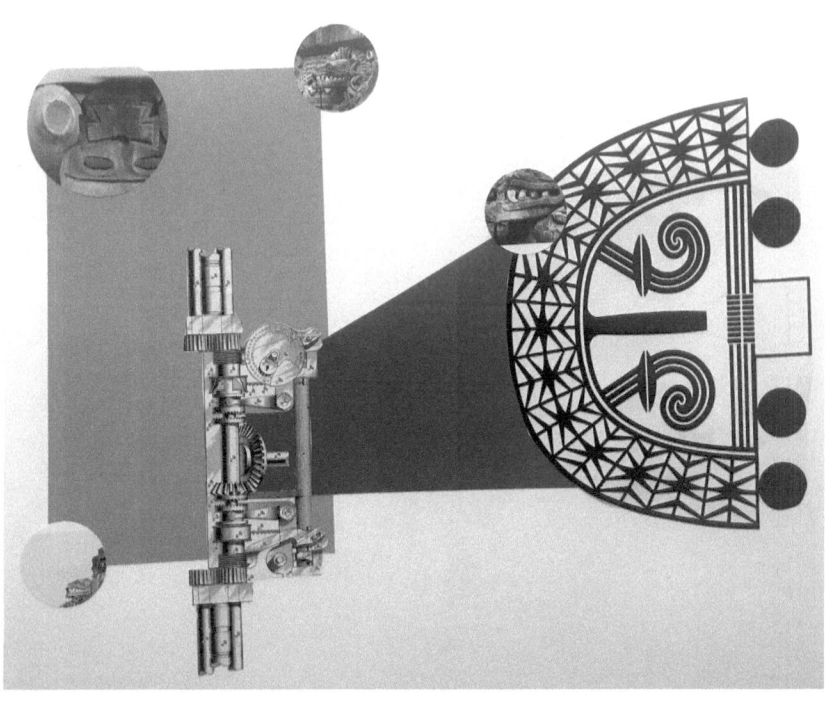

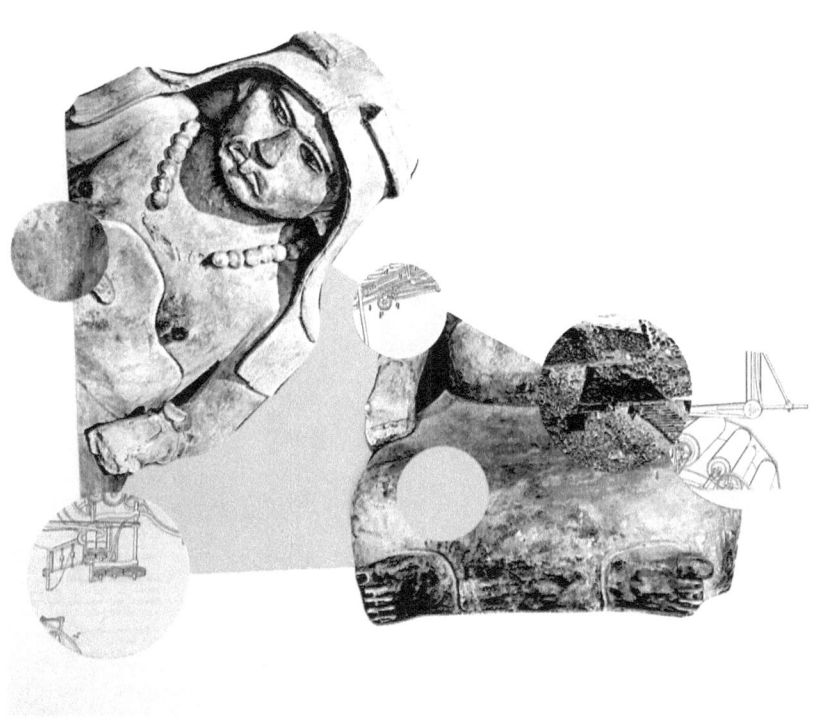

Undeliverable: Returned to Sender

February 21, 2019

Sol LeWitt
Chester, Connecticut

Dear Mr. LeWitt,

I recognize the gross absurdity of writing a letter to you for a number of reasons, not the least being that you are no longer with us. In addition, the idea that an insignificant artist like me addressing someone often described as the most influential American artist of the post-war era feels particularly inappropriate.

But, a few things do motivate me to write. First, because you will never read this letter, I can address you openly without anticipation of a response. I once attended a lecture by art historian Thierry de Duve who spoke of the paradoxical relationship between living artists and those who preceded them. In his view, artists leave a coded message in the form of their work, and years or perhaps decades later, other artists produce works that attempt to engage with that message and perhaps reply to it. Oftentimes, the original artist, belonging to a prior generation, is dead, and it is only their work who survives. The artistic dialogue becomes akin to sending a message into the void to be seen by the living and, hopefully, by later generations, some of who might respond in turn. It is the generational condition of the practice of art. Like me writing to you because I am moved by your work, you were moved by the artists of the Italian Renaissance in a transformative trip you made in 1950 when you first saw the works of Giotto and Pierro della Francesca. You were affected at some point, as I often am, by the work of J.S. Bach, and might have been influenced by his use of seriality and aesthetic. I would like to believe that you took note of these artists' messages and responded to them with your work.

My second reason for writing is that I am fairly certain, had I ever written to you while you were alive, you would have responded independent of the merits or defects of my writing. You would have replied because you had the discipline and moral obligation to do so, because you believed in communication amongst artists, regardless of their status. You were immensely generous. I know of your letters to Eva Hesse, which, in my mind, are some of the most inspiring letters of advice and support given to any artist immersed in the self-doubt that often consumes us. This is perhaps why I decided to write you a letter, even knowing there was no hope of ever receiving a response.

While I never attempted to contact you in life, I have a friend, David Greg Harth, who did so. He wrote to invite you to participate in an art project in which he invited famous people to sign a copy of the Holy Bible. Most never bothered to reply, but you did. You sent a letter saying you would be in New York at some point and hoped to connect. Eventually, he went to your home in Connecticut. You were kind enough to receive him and showed him your studio. He has a photo of you signing his Bible. I find this remarkable. I am not certain whether I would have been as obliging. Yours is a kind of generosity all of us should learn, especially in this art world of posturing and status building.

What I have recently learned about your early years has resonated with me. So, not without humility and a bit of unease, I feel the need to tell you a bit about myself in hopes of articulating something about my education as an artist.

I am lucky in that I was born into a family of artists, (mostly classical musicians) in a house in Colonia Napoles, in Mexico City. It was, and continues to be, a perfectly average middle class Latin American neighborhood, with mostly un-remarkable buildings constructed in the 1950's and 60's. As a child, I drew cartoons and even happened to win a children's art competition or two. When I was twelve, my grandmother took me to Guadalajara to see the murals of Jose Clemente Orozco. That experience cemented my decision to become an artist.

I went home and, instead of drawing cartoons, started to draw large muscular bodies engaging in some kind of struggle. I wasn't sure what struggle my art would depict. I only knew that I wanted to depict one. Somehow, I instinctively felt that art needed to express something important about the human condition.

Down the road from my family's house was the Poliforum Siqueiros, which housed the largest mural in the world and a small basement bookstore. The bookstore was barely visited by anyone, and was somewhat abandoned, as an afterthought of culture. It had musty, brown carpets. But to me it was a wonderful station of learning—the one thing that was accessible to me at the time. It was there where I purchased volumes of Mexican poetry, art history, literature, a book of art manifestos by Siqueiros, and a book of Diego Rivera's writings about art. Those readings were key to my education as an artist.

I tell you this because, a few months ago, I was at the New Britain Museum of American Art doing research when a staff member showed me an old copy of a book about Jewish History entitled *In the Days of the Second Temple*, originally printed in 1929. Around 1941, your thirteen-year-old-self borrowed this book from the local library and, it appears, never returned it. Instead, you filled it with scribbles and cartoons and signed your name and dated it: Sol LeWitt, 1941 A.D.

I was excited to learn that we both shared a passion for reading and making cartoons in our youth. I would like to believe the New Britain Museum played a role in your artistic education in the same way the Poliforum influenced me, as small embassies where the seeds of art were planted in our consciousness.

I am pretty sure that your reserved and private persona would never have had much enthusiasm for the work of an artist that was as overtly political as Siqueiros. And yet, a few months ago at the New Britain Museum, I encountered two of your paintings from your very early years, including a painting of what appears to be a homeless African-American man playing a banjo on a street corner. It vaguely reminds me of Picasso's "The Old Guitarist." If I'm not mistaken, you were probably influenced by the work of social realist artists of the period which, in turn, were influenced by Mexican muralists like Siqueiros. Your painting, in particular, offers a very empathetic look at the disenfranchised and dispossessed. I know that you knew this world, growing up in New Britain during the tail end of the Depression.

Something peculiar happens to us in those formative years. Art becomes our weapon, or our instrument, to modify the course of our initial direction. At times, this means taking the exact opposite course of what was expected. You understood this, saying,

> *I reached the point in high school where I had to go away to school, and by that time I had gotten to the point where it wasn't so much that I wanted to be an artist, it was just that I couldn't stand the life of the town, of this society. I just couldn't. It was more an act of rebellion I think than a positive act of wanting to be an artist . . .*

Like you, I left my hometown to become an artist. I remember being told by a friend that I would never return. I adamantly denied it, dismissing her comment as ridiculous. There was no doubt in my mind that my schooling in the U.S. would be brief, and that I would return in a few years. But, her words were prophetic. I have been away from Mexico for thirty years now. I return for visits and share a special bond with local artists and other friends there, but I have made a life outside of Mexico and do not see myself ever returning for good. It is perhaps an urge to embrace the role of the artist as an outsider, of getting out of our familiar reality so we can see with greater clarity.

Our relationship with our hometown is always complex. I love Mexico City and continue to derive enormous inspiration from it. At the same time, the city exasperates me. I lose my temper with its bureaucracy, its chaos, and the way it consumes me. I suspect your feelings toward your origins may have been different. You returned to Connecticut and bequeathed many works of art to the museum, the very one in which people are now reading my letter to you. The museum that gave you one of your first museum group shows. The one which has in its collection the aforementioned book with your juvenalia, and at least two paintings from your early period that have been seemingly overlooked by art historians.

I am pretty sure you probably would not have liked seeing these paintings survive and I suspect that you would have disowned them had you encountered them later in life. But, to me, these are valuable works that speak to your character. Even if your practice remained committed to formal and conceptual frameworks, and even though your works were conceived as autonomous entities not meant to directly comment on the real world in the way social realism does, I am certain the spirit of empathy and generosity always remained in you, in the way you freely exchanged works and letters with other artists, and in the way you supported and recognized the possibilities of other practices, even if they were radically different from yours.

Your work and your life have taught me there is much more to an artist than the artwork. Perhaps a lot of what happens in our lives should remain private. I am too aware of the desire to read biography into someone's artwork, something I call the "Van Gogh Syndrome." Not all our life experiences translate into art works, or even influences of our work. To assume too much can be dangerous and force unfair or inaccurate interpretations.

The other day, I saw a photograph of the house you grew up in. I felt the same fascination as I have always felt by being at the birth homes or the living spaces of other artists and recognized our need to project meaning to those physical spaces, imagine stories behind every object that belonged to the artist, to give them some kind of religious meaning due to the devotion we have to the works these artists produced.

Looking at your childhood home, I had a thought:

Artists are outsiders. We look into the world and make objects, gestures that speak to it. But we are sometimes outsiders to ourselves, as well. We can be outsiders of our own biographies. We take all we have lived and learned and use it for our craft, our language. But, in the end, what we create is another individual, the one who makes the work. Borges said it best when he wrote it is the condition of self-outsider-ness that keeps us alive, that truly makes us artists. I think you were someone who didn't want the person and the artwork to become blended.

I suspect we can also become outsiders of our own works. I remember reading a text of yours where you argued that artists should always retain the right to transform their work. I have thought for many years about that and believe that once the work leaves our hands, it needs to live a life of its own. Our desire to transform it can result in erasing the past simply to create new work. More than a curse, I find that liberating. Like letting our children live their own lives. If we ever had met in person, I would have probably liked to speak to you about this.

I write this letter in a tiny hotel room in a foreign city as I prepare to attend an opening that will offer plenty of what you once referred to as "vertical torture." I would rather stay here, writing to you, or to the memory of you, or to the unresponsive void, depending how one sees it. I am happy, however, for the time being, to continue trying to decode the messages you left behind, hoping also that, one day, someone who I will never get to meet might also receive my letters.

Yours truly,

Pablo Helguera

APPENDIX

Variations on a Childhood Home

(for Sol LeWitt)

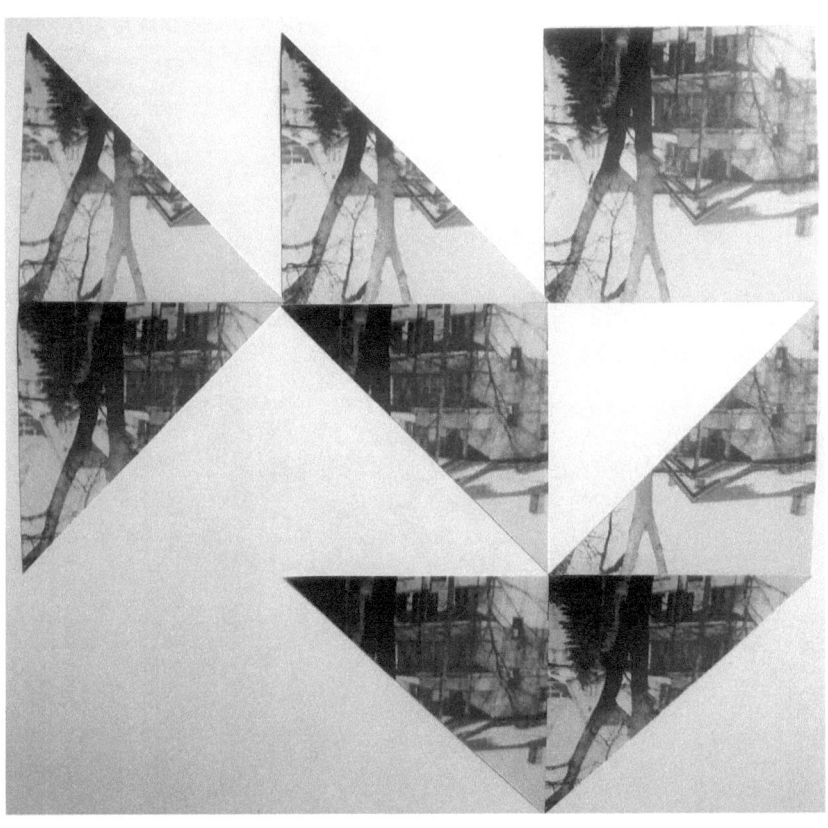

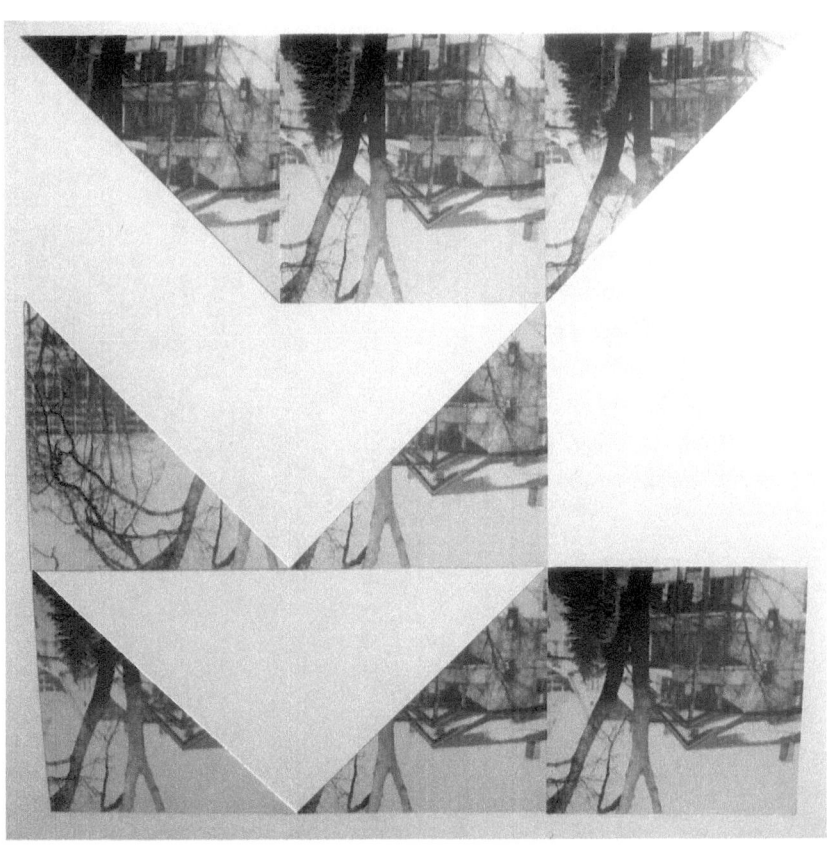

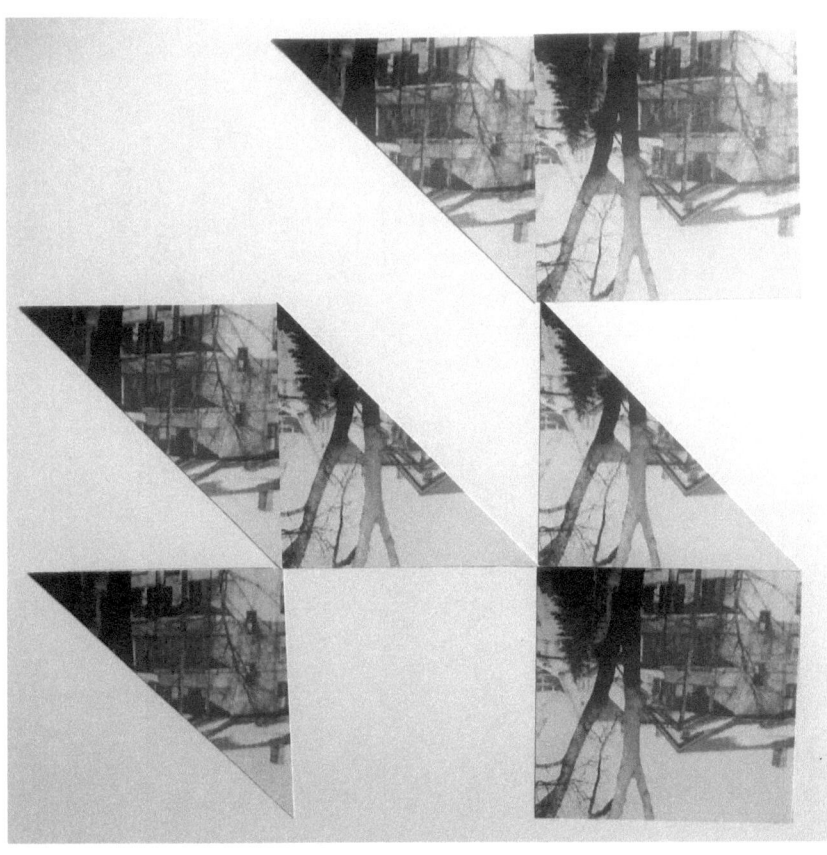

About the Author

In a methodical way and recurring to strategies connected to the baroque fugue and ars combinatoria (combinatory art), Pablo Helguera (Mexico City, 1971) often draws improbable relationships between human histories, biographies, anecdotes and historical events, always bringing them all together in a cohesive whole and making all serve as a reflection on our current relationship with art as a society. Helguera often focuses on history, pedagogy, sociolinguistics and anthropology in formats such as lectures, museum displays, performance and written fiction. His project *The School of Panamerican Unrest* (2003-2011), an early example of pedagogically-focused socially engaged art, consisted in a nomadic think-tank, physically crossed the continent by car from Anchorage to Tierra del Fuego. He has exhibited and performed widely (MoMA, Havana Biennial, Performa, Reina Sofia, amongst many others) and has been recipient of the Guggenheim, Franklin Furnace and Blade of Grass Fellowships and the Creative Capital and Art Matters grants. He was the first recipient of the International Award of Participatory Art of the Emilia Romagna Region in Italy. His book *Education for Socially Engaged Art*, (2011), a primer for social practice has quickly become adopted as a main textbook for art schools and university programs internationally. He is also author of several other books including *The Pablo Helguera Manual of Contemporary Art Style, Theatrum Anatomicum (and other performance lectures)*, *What in the World*, and *Art Scenes: The Social Scripts of the Art World*, a book on the sociology of contemporary art. In 2013 he launched the project *Librería Donceles*, consisting in creating the only Spanish used bookstore in New York, a non-profit project intended to draw attention to the perceptions of Latin American culture in the U.S. Since 2007, he is Director of Adult and Academic Programs in the Education Department of the Museum of Modern Art in New York. Currently, the Jumex Museum in Mexico City is presenting a multi-year mid-career retrospective of his work under the title *Dramatis Personae*.

Other books by Pablo Helguera
also published by Jorge Pinto Books:

Endingness: Prolegomena for a New Art of Memory
The Pablo Helguera Manual of Contemporary Art Style
The Boy Inside the Letter
The Witches of Tepoztlán (and Other Unpublished Operas)
Artoons (I, II, and *III)*
The Juvenal Players
Suite Panamericana
Hacia una Estética de la Burocracia
Estela y las Hojas
Theatrum Anatomicum (and Other Performance Lectures)
The Juvenal Players
What in the World (a Subjective Museum Biography)
The School of Panamerican Unrest (an Anthology of Documents)—
    with Sara Demeuse
Urÿonstelaii
Education for Socially Engaged Art
Art Scenes: The Social Scripts of the Art World
Onda Corta
He Was Elan
An Atlas of Commonplaces
La lección de Anatomía del profesor Acirema